GROLIER
Your partner in education

**Distributed by Grolier, Sherman Turnpike
Danbury, Connecticut 06816**

Grolier offers a varied selection of
children's book racks and tote bags.
For details on ordering, please write:
Grolier Direct Marketing
Sherman Turnpike
Danbury, CT 06816
Att: Premium Department

My **W** Book

by Jane Belk Moncure

illustrated by Linda Hohag

THE CHILD'S WORLD

Mankato, MN 56001

Little  had a

She said, "I will fill my  box.

I will put my wildcat

and my wand into my box."

Little  put on her hat and cape.

"I will be a good witch," she said.

She found a

woodpecker

and wiggly worms.
She put them into
her box.

Little  found

a weasel.

He wiggled into the box.

A wolf was

after him.

box

Little  waved her wand.

"Wolf, be good," she said.
Guess where she put the wolf?

Little **W** found a well.

It was a wishing well. "I wish ...

I wish I had something bigger for my things," said

Little w.

Little w found a wheelbarrow.

Away
she went...

down the road
to the water.

"I will wade in the water,"
she said.

"Wow," said a walrus.
"What a wacky witch."

Little **w** said,

"You belong in my box,
walrus."

Little  put the walrus into the box.

The walrus winked at the wolf.

box

Little  went back to the water.

A whale was in the water.

"You are so big," said Little W.

Little found a wagon,

a big, big wagon.

Away she went, right into a . . .

wall.

What was behind
the wall?

Watermelons.

"Let's have a watermelon party," said Little W.

watermelons

wheelbarrow

wiggly worms

wall

water

wishing well

whale

walrus

weasel

wagon

wolf

wildcat

And they did.

More words with Little

woman

window

web

watch

wallet

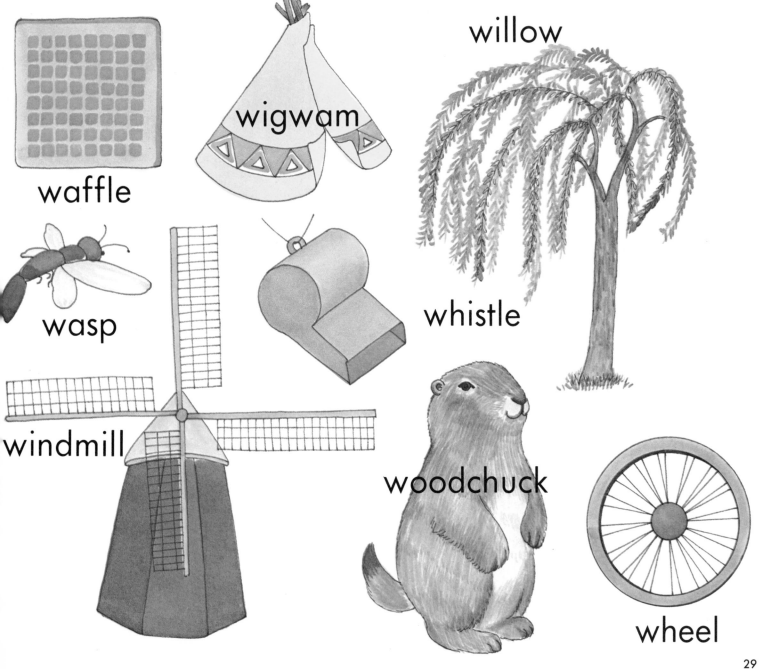

waffle

wigwam

willow

wasp

whistle

windmill

woodchuck

wheel